This book belongs to

....

I give it

★ ★ ★
★
★ ★ ★
★
★ ★

stars

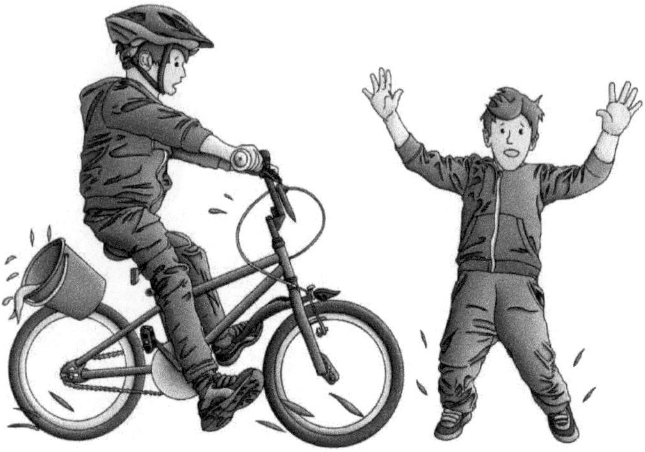

BILLY HELPS MAX

BILLY GROWING UP SERIES: STEALING

JAMES MINTER

Helen Rushworth - Illustrator

www.billygrowingup.com

MINTER PUBLISHING LIMITED

Minter Publishing Limited (MPL)
4 Lauradale
Bracknell RG12 7DT

Copyright © James Minter 2016

James Minter has asserted his rights under the Copyright, Design, and Patents Act, 1988 to be the author of this work

Paperback ISBN: 978-1-910727-18-8
Hardback ISBN: 978-1-910727-20-1
eBook ISBN: 978-1-910727-19-5

Illustrations copyright © Helen Rushworth

Printed and bound in Great Britain by Ingram Spark, Milton Keynes

This book is sold subject to the condition that it shall not, by way of trade or otherwise, be lent, resold, hired out, or otherwise circulated in any form of binding or cover other than that in which it is published and without a similar condition, including this condition, being imposed on the subsequent purchaser.

>>>>>

DEDICATED to those who think stealing is acceptable. They are so wrong.

<<<<<

1

IT'S NOT FAIR

"It's not fair!" Max said as she threw her bike to the ground. "Why won't you let me have a go?" She stormed off.

Ant looked, first, at his sister then at his best mate Billy. Both boys shrugged as they watched her walk across the lawn heading toward the backdoor.

The boys were kneeling in Ant's garden as they built a bike ramp out of two wooden planks—the type used by workmen when putting up scaffolding—

and an upturned metal bucket. One end of each plank rested on the ground while the other rested on the bucket. It seemed like a good idea; however, every time they tried to ride up the slope, the planks toppled off.

For the umpteenth time, Ant laid the planks back on the bucket, and now he was determined to secure them in place. He hurried off to look for extra support. Reaching his dad's shed, Ant disappeared inside. Amongst the tools, the lawn mower, and other Dad stuff, and after several bangs, clatters, and the use of words neither his mother nor Miss Tompkins, his form teacher, would tolerate, Ant re-emerged carrying four house bricks left over from the building of the garden wall.

Between strides, he announced, "This should do it." He looked at his mate.

Billy, sat on his bike at the far side of the garden, waiting for Ant to place the bricks under the planks. After a few minutes, Ant gave him the thumbs up.

Billy raised himself off his seat and used his whole body weight to push down on the pedals. The bike lurched forward. With each rotation of the chain-wheel, it gained speed. Focussed on the ramp, and confident he would hit it square on, he went for the big one. *This is it.* He told himself. *Ant will be so impressed.* The wind blew in his face, and his helmet wobbled from side to side as he rode as hard as he could.

Ant squatted on his haunches to get a better view of the wheels striking the ramp. Since he wanted to build a slope that lasted, Ant needed to see what kept going wrong.

With both boys concentrating on the task, neither of them noticed that Ant's sister Max hadn't made it to the backdoor. Her anger had reached boiling point. Instead, she turned and ran as fast as she could back toward the ramp. *If they won't let me play, then they won't play either.* The thought drove her on. Max reached the first plank with only seconds to spare. Without stopping, she kicked at the wood, sending it off the bucket and clattering to the ground.

The front wheel of Billy's bike arrived where the jump should have been. With no ramp, he flew straight ahead, catching his bike's pedal in the handle of the spinning bucket. The bike swung violently off course, and now Billy headed directly toward the shed. Both boy and bike might have faced total disaster if it hadn't been for Ant crouched in between.

Ant's instant response came automatically; he leapt like a frightened frog away from the path of the speeding bike. He rolled to a stop. Billy did not and hit the shed door with a loud bang.

"Max! Why on Earth did you do that?" Ant dusted himself down before jumping up and running after his sister. She had made it to the bottom of the garden and the gate that led out into the lane behind their house.

"'Cos you said I couldn't have a go," she shouted over her shoulder while she ran down the hill.

"But you're a girl, and this is boy's stuff. Anyway, your bike is too prissy." Ant watched her until she ran out of sight. "Where are you going?" he called after her.

Either she didn't hear or chose not to answer. Ant turned and wandered back to Billy.

"You all right?" Ant gave Billy a slap on the back before setting about rebuilding the ramp.

Katie, Max's fifth best friend, lived only two streets away. The lane behind Max's house gave a quick and safe shortcut between their houses. Arriving at the backdoor, Max twisted the handle. Even though there was no one around, Max let herself in as she often did. Just as she crossed the threshold, Eddy—Katie's older brother—came up behind her. He barged passed, knocking the door out of her hand and grunting as he did.

"What do you want?" Eddy didn't stop walking.

Max spoke in a small, mouse-like voice, "Katie."

"Who?"

"Katie. Is she here?"

"No idea. Don't care." He strode off into the house. "Katie," he hollered at the top of his voice before disappearing upstairs.

Max felt unsure of what to do. She stood half in and half out of the backdoor. Then she tilted her head to one side, hoping to hear sounds of Katie approaching. She waited, even holding her breath to hear better, but no sound reached her. After a couple of minutes, she thought it best to leave. Max didn't want to go up to Katie's bedroom as usual, in case she met *him* on the stairs or in the hallway or some other place. Eddy scared her and he was nearly twice her age. Max didn't like to feel scared except at the funfair when she rode the ghost train.

BILLY HELPS MAX 11

Max decided to leave and pulled the door closed behind her. She rotated the handle until it clicked shut; she was trying not to make a noise. With the door properly secure, she twisted herself around to walk off. As she did, she came face-to-face with Katie.

"Oh!" Katie had surprised her. "Don't do that." Max took a gasp of air and patted her chest to get her breath back. "You really scared me."

"Sorry, Max, I didn't mean to. I've just been to the shops for Mum. She wanted a loaf of bread." Katie held it up. "So, what are you doing here? Why didn't you go up to my bedroom like normal?"

"Eddy." Max whispered as she looked

around to see if he lurked nearby.

"Don't take any notice of him." Both girls went inside. "He makes loads of noise, but he's okay, really. Fancy an orange juice?"

Max said nothing. Staring straight ahead she seemed distant as if in a dream.

"You okay, Max?" Katie came up to her and looked directly into her face. "What's wrong?"

"It's my brother and Billy." Max cast her eyes downward.

"What do you mean?"

"They've been nasty to me."

"Have you told your mum?" Katie sounded concerned.

"They won't let me play with them."

Max sniffed as she spoke.

Katie tried to console her, "My brothers are like that."

"You're just saying that. Tom's nice. I bet he's not nasty, and Eddy's too old."

Katie passed Max a glass of orange. "Come on, let's go up to my bedroom. We don't need boys." Katie led the way. "I've got Connect-Four and a Mr. Potato Head." She ran up the stairs.

"Your two brothers—" Max followed Katie. "—don't you play with them?"

"Not really. Well, not Eddy, anyway. When I was a lot younger, he played hide and seek with me, but that was years ago. Tom, maybe; he's nearer my age." She dropped a yellow counter into the Connect-

Four frame.

"Wouldn't you like to do what they do?" Max asked.

Katie scrunched up her eyes, "What do you mean?"

"Skateboarding, or going down the woods on your bike, or acting out Star Wars battles; you know, boy's stuff."

"Yeah, but we've got dressing up, playing shop, or being mummies with our dolls. Anyway, I'm sure we could do boys things if we wanted to." Katie didn't look up; instead, she sat concentrating on her next Connect-Four move.

"Ant says my bike is too pretty or something like that. It's so pink, and it's got a basket and mudguards."

"But that's good if it rains isn't it?" Katie dropped another counter into the Connect-Four frame.

"I don't go out when it rains, and I hardly ever use my basket." Max's eyes glazed over as she thought about how she could make her bike more like a boy's. "That's it! I'll show them." Max jumped up and headed out of the bedroom. "See ya."

Kate dropped her counter. "What, yeah, okay."

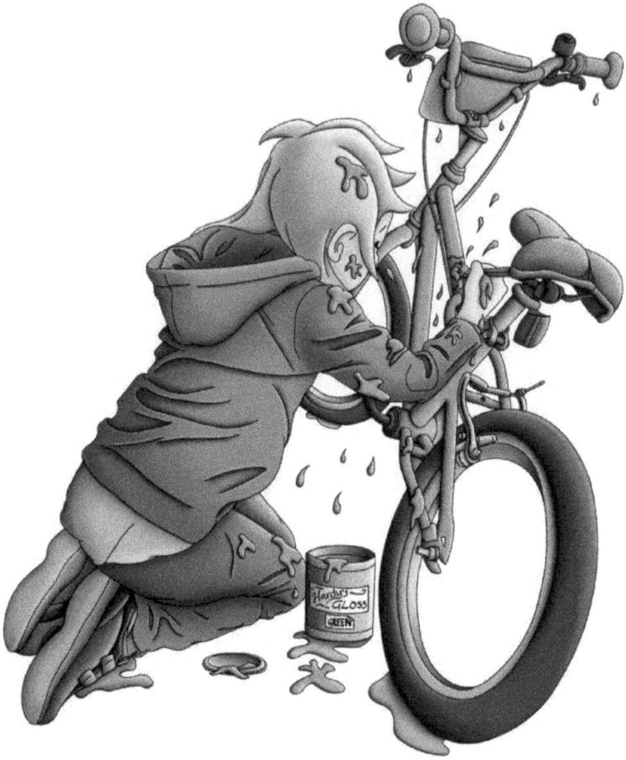
Hardy's
GLOSS
GREEN

2

NO LONGER A PRISSY BIKE

Max reached the back gate to her garden and peeked over to see where Ant and Billy were. *Good, they must still be messing about with that ramp.* She watched for a few minutes as Ant nailed bits of wood between the planks going around the outside of the bucket while Billy held them in place.

Taking her chances, Max slipped through the gate and headed for her dad's shed hopefully unnoticed. She walked in a large semi-circle to keep well away from the boys in case they chased her. Once inside she ducked down; hidden, Max viewed the boys for another minute.

At the sound of the shed door closing, Ant looked over. "Don't ask," he said to Billy. "I've no idea what she's doing."

Billy passed him another nail; Ant swung the heavy hammer. It made a loud bang each time he hit the nail, and an even louder clang when he missed and hit the bucket instead.

In the shed, Max rummaged through her dad's tools. She had no idea what she needed but picked up a screwdriver and adjustable spanner. Fascinated, she spun the spanner's thumbscrew, watching the jaws open and close in response.

All I need now is my bike. Bent at the waist to avoid being seen, Max made her way to the shed window. Still crouched, she peered out. Her bike lay where she had thrown it earlier. Both boys remained intent on nailing up the ramp. This was her chance. Max edged open the door. It made a squeak. "Shush," she whispered as she squeezed through the narrow gap. Once outside, she ran. Then, snatching up her bike she dragged it back to the shed before the boys saw.

With the door shut firmly, Max got to work. Her first task was to remove the basket by undoing the two brown leather straps holding it to the handlebars. She laid the basket in a space on one of the many shelves, not wanting to throw it away—just in case.

Already, her bike looked different, less girly, but not suitable for taking down to the woods. Max smiled at what she saw. "Good job".

With her tongue pressed into her cheek, she got to work on the front mudguard. To remove it, she picked up both the screwdriver and spanner. After several tries, she unscrewed the thin wire stays that stopped the mudguard from wobbling. All that remained was a nut and bolt holding the mudguard to the bike's forks. Though awkward, Max eventually managed to loosen it but her fingers got incredibly mucky. After slipping out the mudguard from between the forks, she placed it alongside the basket.

Now for the hard part. Max rattled the rear-mudguard. It was held in place by four difficult-to-get-at screws and bolts.

"Ouch." She looked at the back of her hand; her scraped knuckles bled, but that didn't dampen her determination to finish the job. After a lot more effort, dirt and scratches, Max finally removed the rear mudguard.

Her bike looked different, less girly and more the sort of thing a boy would ride — though it remained very pink. Max beamed. *I need something to cover up the colour.* With that thought, she turned her attention to finding some paint.

The shed had several shelves of paint tins all jumbled up by size and colour. Max's experience of paints was limited to watercolours used at school, and not grown-up paints used for decorating houses. She had no idea of the difference between gloss or matt, interior or exterior, single coat or undercoat. Or that these paints didn't wash off with water, but required a special weird smelling liquid called white spirit to remove any spills.

All that interested her was the colour, and her dad had a rainbow of colours. She liked yellow because it looked like the sun, and she saw the tin of her bedroom-pink paint, but chose to ignore both, hoping to find something more boyish. Max gazed at the shelves until a different colour caught her eye.

Attracted by an emerald green label, she lifted down the tin to get a better look.

"What about this one?" she said to herself. "It's definitely not pink or yellow." She walked the tin over to the window to study it in daylight.

As she passed the bench Max picked up a screwdriver and slipped the flat end between the edge of the lid and the tin. Then, pushing down, the lid lifted enough so she could see the colour inside. "Awesome." Satisfied it was the right colour, she flipped the lid off completely. It trundled across the bench and fell onto the floor, leaving a bright green trail of fresh paint as it went.

Curious, Max pushed her finger into the tin. The contents felt thick, not runny like water, but more like green custard. She sniffed at it.

"Poo, that's disgusting. It certainly doesn't smell like custard." Max wiped her green finger across the leg of her jeans until it appeared clean. When she held up her hand to check, she noticed the paint on her fingernail. *What would I look like if I painted all my nails? Probably a witch.* She let out a cackle, and then hushed herself in case the boys heard. "Right, I need a brush."

Her dad had an assortment of brushes—from super thin ones, used for painting pictures, to great fat ones so wide they would not fit into the tin. She chose a size suitable for the emerald green tin, but not too small, or it would take ages to paint her bike.

Pushing the brush into the paint until the bristles disappeared below the surface Max pulled it slowly out. Not wanting to make a mess, she held the brush, bristles upwards. By the time she reached her bike, much of the paint had run down the handle and onto her hand, leaving it green, as well as onto her jumper sleeve, turning it into a gooey mess.

Quickly, with each brush stroke, the bike changed colour. Not a smooth, even green, but more a patchy green like army camouflage with streaks of pink showing through. The black tyres plus the chrome of the handlebars and wheel rims took on a similar look. Even the once cream-coloured saddle didn't escape her attention.

With all the bending and bobbing, Max's blonde hair fell forward across her face. "Bother." With a single flick of her hand, the one holding the brush, she removed the offending hair. In the process, she gave herself a green parting, running from her fringe to the top of her head.

She stood back to admire her new, less girly bike with its unique paint job. *All I need now,* she thought, *are go-faster stripes. … Wait 'til Ant sees my bike.*

Thinking of Ant reminded her of the boys. Listening, she realised the hammering had stopped. From the shed window neither Ant nor his bike were in sight, but she could see Billy seated with his back to the shed studying the ramp.

"They cannot stop me now." Max had stubbornness in her voice, although no one could hear. Her grin broadened to fill her whole face.

"Okay, I'll count you down." Billy raised his arm.

Ant sat on his bike with one foot resting on a pedal and the other on the ground.

"Three … two … one." Billy dropped his arm.

Ant pushed off. His bike shot forward. Standing, he pedalled fast and furious. The speed increased, the front wheel hit the ramp, everything stayed in place, and both wheels now travelled along the plank.

Ant pushed his hardest when he felt the front of his bike rise up. He yanked hard on the handlebars to make the most of the upward thrust. The front wheel rose into the air, closely followed by the back. Not exactly flying, but he did manage an impressive jump. He landed well over a meter beyond the ramp, and more importantly, the planks remained in place.

"Epic." Ant punched the air before turning around for another go. He didn't stop moving, and as soon as the ramp came into view, he let rip. His pace and determination increased. With his chin resting on the handlebars to reduce wind drag, he pedalled so fast that his feet became a blur.

At the same time, although the paint on Max's bike felt nowhere near dry, she wanted to show it off.

Opening the shed door, Max called out at the top of her voice, "Billy, Ant, here."

Taken by surprise, both boys spun around. The distraction came just as Ant's front wheel met the leading plank of the ramp. He lost concentration; the bike veered off the ramp, over the path, and straight into the concrete steps leading up to the back door. The bike stopped dead.

The energy which had built up in the moving bicycle had to go somewhere; it transferred to Ant. He lost grip of the handlebars and flew. Grabbing at thin air he tried to save himself. With his arms flapping he looked more like someone just fired from a circus cannon—a human cannonball—but without a safety net.

Airborne only for a few seconds, he shot across the garden, landing face down into the flowerbed in front of the newly built garden wall.

Billy stood, fixed to the spot; he didn't know what to do. Max's green bike grabbed his attention, but so did a flying Ant.

"Max!" Billy shouted before turning

back. "Ant!"

Ant won, and Billy dashed the length of the garden to his friend. "You okay?" He bent down to lift Ant's face out of the dark, squelchy, freshly manured soil.

Even with his face caked in muck, Ant managed a smile. He tried to speak, "Me … flying …" but instead he swallowed a nasty something, which he then coughed up quickly; he spat several times.

Max arrived alongside them without her bike.

"Sorry, Ant." His sister sounded sheepish, "I just wanted to show you my painted bike."

Both boys gawped at her. Their mouths fell open, and their eyes never blinked.

"What?" Max patted herself down. "Why are you staring at me like that?"

Billy stood and turned her toward the back door. Reflected in the glass pane, she could see herself covered from head to toe in splashes, streaks, daubs, and dribbles of green paint.

"We use paint at school all the time." Max sounded unconcerned, "It's easy to wash off."

"Not this. It's gloss," Billy said.

"What's gloss?"

"What you're covered in. Gloss paint doesn't wash off." Billy sounded serious.

Max felt a tear in the corner of her eye. *No, she mustn't cry. Only babies cry.* Hoping that Billy hadn't seen, she wiped her tear away with her soggy sleeve. It left a large green smear from her eye to her chin.

"Stop. You're making it worse." Billy pointed out the new stripe. "I need to help Ant; you stay here and touch nothing. I'll be back"

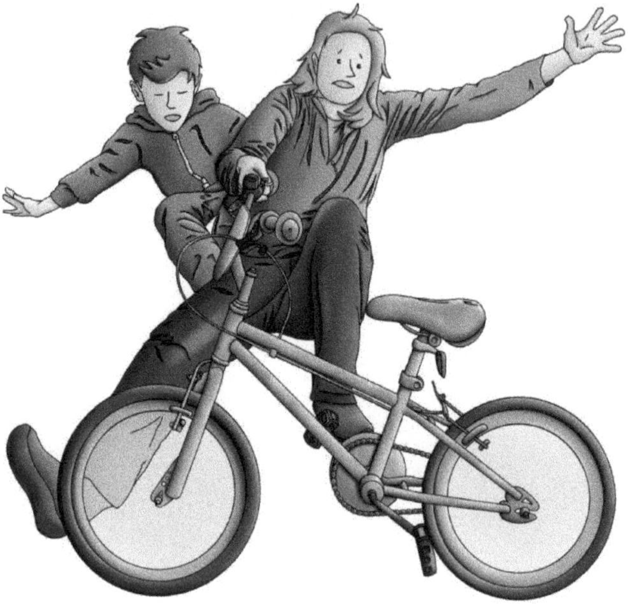

3

YOU CAN'T LET MUM SEE YOU

"Max, you can't let your mum see you like that; she'll go ballistic. ... Just look at you, and your bike." Billy turned to Ant, "And you need to wash your face; landing in that muck can't be nice." He took his friend by the arm and led him toward the kitchen. Turning to Max he said, "Remember, touch nothing—promise." Billy stared at her until she nodded.

"Where's your mum?" Billy asked Ant.

They both looked around, hoping not to see her.

"I think she's in the spare bedroom—" Ant spat as he spoke. "—doing some spring cleaning." When he talked, it caused his jaw muscles to move, dislodging more muck; he spat again. Ant wiped at his face. Billy walked toward the back door while Ant hobbled along behind.

When they reached the steps, Ant lifted a leg. "Ouch, my knee hurts really badly." He sat and rubbed it.

"Yeah, but we've got to get your face clean." Billy lifted Ant and pulled him into a standing position. "Come on; I've got to get you cleaned up, and your sister." Billy looked beyond Ant and noticed Max wiping her face. "Max, stop! You're spreading paint everywhere; take off your jumper."

Billy helped Ant through the back door and into the kitchen. "Here." He handed him several sheets of paper towel. "Now, stick your face under the tap; I'll help Max." He turned to leave, "And listen out for your mum. Don't let her come out to the shed."

"Why not?" Ant had forgotten about his paint-covered sister.

"Because I need to clean up Max," Billy called back as he ran. "Look at the state of her." He sprinted across the lawn, "Come on, Max, we need to get you into your dad's shed." As Billy passed he bent and picked up her jumper, making sure not to touch any of the painted areas..

Max's bike was resting against the outside wall of the shed with its front wheel blocking the doorway. Billy wanted to avoid getting any green gloss on himself so he placed one finger from one hand under the handlebar stem, and a second finger from his other hand near the saddle, to push the bike away from the entrance. He swung the shed door open and saw inside for the first time.

"Flipping heck!" Billy couldn't hide his surprise. "I'll never ask you to paint my bike." The wooden floorboards were soaked in paint.

"Well, how should I know it was grass paint?" Max blushed, although Billy couldn't see because of the green spatters and streaks covering her face.

"Gloss, not grass; though, it's the right colour." Billy studied the floor, looking for a path across to where he could see shelves of glass bottles and jars. "Have you seen any white spirit?"

"I've seen white paint; Dad used it on all our doors. He let me cover my bedroom in stickers. I like stickers." Max smiled at the thought, and then picked up an old bit of cloth and rubbed at her fingers.

"There's no point doing that without white spirit; the green won't come off." Billy took a step to the left to avoid the tacky green tyre marks made when Max rolled out her bike. He stopped to work out his next move. For certain, he didn't want to get his nearly new and his favourite trainers covered in green paint.

Up on tiptoe, he took a step forward. Then he lost his balance and toppled toward a particularly large pool of paint next to where the tin lay on its side. He leapt to avoid stepping in it. With a loud thud, he landed, and all the glass containers rattled, and several looked as if they might fall. Still moving forward, he swung his arms up, ready to catch them. Unable to stop himself, he crashed into the bench. Three jars shook before starting to fall.

Max sat on the only clean patch of floor big enough to take her. She watched Billy's antics, and clapped him when he caught the glass bottles. "Well done."

"Now, where's the white spirit?" Billy glanced at the shelves.

Max pointed, excited. "There ..., top shelf, along that way."

"Well spotted." Billy stood as tall as he could and reached up, but his fingers proved too short. Instead, he looked around and found a paint-covered stick that Max's dad used for stirring. With the stick in one hand, Billy pushed the bottle off the shelf. It tumbled forward. He caught it with the other hand.

Max gave him another clap. "You're

good at this."

Billy, careful of where he walked, crossed the floor back to Max. With the bottle held upright, he tried to unscrew it. "Stupid child-proof cap." He sighed. "I'll have to get your mum to do it." With three strides, he'd raced from the shed and was out of sight.

"Wow, that was quick," Max said on Billy's return. "What did Mum say?"

"I told her I needed to clean up a paint spill. I didn't tell her how much. ... Where's that rag?"

Billy took the cloth from Max and, holding it at arm's length, dribbled a few drops of white spirit onto it. "Here."

"'Cor, it's super whiffy." Max curled up her nose while she rubbed at her hands. Gradually, eight fingers, two thumbs, and two palms turned from paint green to skin pink. She held them out for inspection.

"You'll need to wash them in soapy water," Billy said. "But, now, we have a bigger problem—your face and hair."

The shed door swung open.

"Max! What on Earth have you done?" The shrill voice of Max's mum made it difficult to understand what she said exactly, but it didn't matter that much. Max knew she was in trouble; deep, deep trouble. Trouble with a capital "T".

Immediately, her eyes welled up, her throat squeezed shut, and her chest tightened. She opened her mouth to speak, but the tremble of her chin meant nothing came out. Fearful and confused, Max stood with head hung low. She wanted her mum to understand, to appreciate how she felt about the boys and their bikes, and what she had done. With her arms outstretched, she ran at her mum.

"No!" Her mum took a large step back to avoid an embrace from her paint-covered daughter.

Hearing all the shouting, Ant had limped across the garden to the shed. Standing right behind his mum he didn't have time to react. In free-fall, their mum crashed backwards grabbing at anything to stop herself. The *anything* was Max's bike.

To make matters worse, she and the bike landed on top of Ant. Both were pinned to the ground; they were stuck.

Max saw this as an opportunity to get away; to escape the telling-off she knew she had coming. After sidestepping, she ran into the garden. *If I could get myself clean, maybe it wouldn't end up so bad.* Once in the kitchen, she remembered what Billy had said about soap and water. She kicked off her shoes and then ran through the house, up the stairs, and into the bathroom, heading for the shower. Max slammed the door so hard that it rattled on its hinges.

🐕 🐕

Billy watched Ant and his mum struggling to get up. He felt awkward and confused as to what to do next. Desperately, he wanted to go home, but getting them from under the bike seemed more important. Billy gathered his courage and collected up the tatty cloth that Max had used to clean her hands before he picked up the bike.

Ant's mum hadn't escaped the curse of the green paint. Multiple stripes marked her clothes, and where she had struggled to get up, she left handprints everywhere.

"Right, my girl, you've not heard the last of this." Ant's mum looked around for Max.

Ant lay on the ground, winded and wheezing. The sounds caught his mum's attention.

"Oh Ant, did I hurt you?" She crouched

beside him. "Speak to me Ant. Are you okay?"

Pulling Ant into a sitting position, she rubbed his back to help him breathe—it did—but it also coated his hoody in green paint. She noticed. "Oh, for goodness sake, that girl's in real trouble." Lifting Ant upright she turned to Billy. "What's been going on? Did you have anything to do with this?"

Arriving at the bathroom door, Max's mum turned the handle and pushed. Nothing happened.

"Max, let me in, *now!*" Her mum pushed harder. "Max!"

The sound of running water reached

Max's mum's ears.

"Did you hear me Max?" Her mum pushed on the door again. The noise of the water stopped. Max's mum stood back from the door and folded her arms across her chest. With her brow furrowed, her eyebrows met in the middle, her nostrils flared like a charging bull, and she held her mouth so wide open, ready to blast her daughter, that it looked like an entrance to a cave. She appeared fearsome.

Max inched the door ajar, and her head came into view.

"Crikeyyyyy!" Her mum made the same noise a cartoon cat does when its tail gets stood on. She looked much the same, too. If she had fur, it would have stood on end, and like paws, her arms shot out in pure astonishment before she clasped her hands to her face.

Instead of seeing her lovely eight-year-old daughter with her mass of blonde curls, freckled face, and blue eyes, and wearing an ear-to-ear smile, her mum saw what looked like a two-year-old child's drawing of a monster from planet Mars. What remained of Max's hair stood upright, stiff with green paint. The rest lay on the bathroom floor like a garden lawn before the grass cuttings get raked away. Wrapped in her mum's new, for special occasions only, luxurious white bath towel, the paint, soap, and water mixture added an unwelcome collection of green stripes.

The shock of seeing Max silenced her mum. She had no clue of what to do or say, and her eyes filled with tears. What she wanted was to grab hold of Max to make things better. Dumb struck, she could only gawp.

Eventually, Max's mum found her voice, "Right, my girl, back into that shower and make sure you don't touch anything."

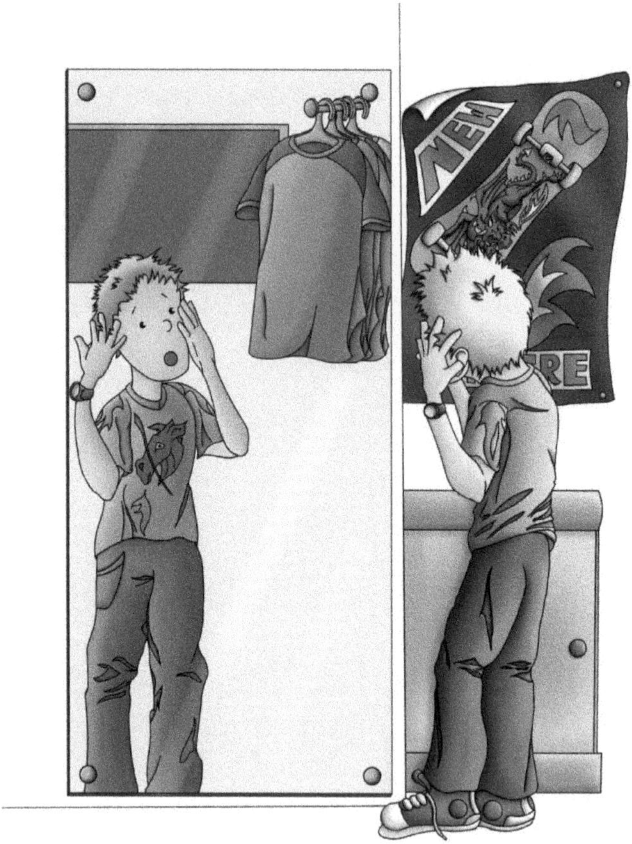
NEW

4

AT THE HAIRDRESSER

"Sorry, Ant, I had to send Billy home. We need to get Max a haircut, and the hairdresser could only do it this afternoon." Max's mum looked at her watch, "A bus will come by shortly." She picked up her handbag and door key. "Come on you two, quickly."

"But, Mum, I can't go out looking like this." Max pulled her jacket collar up, trying to hide inside it.

"You should have thought about that

before you painted your head."

"I didn't mean to, it just sort of happened. My hair flopped in front of my eyes, and I flicked it out of the way with the brush." Another tear rolled down Max's cheek.

"Well, it won't flop again, and certainly not after the visit to the hairdressers." Max's mum remained unsympathetic.

The bus stopped outside the shopping centre.

"Quickly, now." Their mum shepherded them off the bus, smiling politely at the people staring at Max and mumbling "hairdresser" to anyone listening.

"What happened, Mrs Turner?" The

hairdresser's shock seemed clear. "The colour, the cut, her skin, where's your pretty daughter gone?"

"That's a long story but, as you can imagine, I feel very unhappy with her. Please see what you can do to make her less ..." She looked at her daughter while she thought of the right word, "... green!"

The hairdresser took Max and sat her in a large black swivel chair facing a wall of mirrors. Stood behind Max, the hairdresser walked, first, to one side before trying to push her fingers through the green mat of hair and failing. She then tried the other side with no success. She shook her head. "Not sure what to do, Mrs Turner." She rubbed her chin while thinking some more.

"Baby oil," said a woman sitting in the next chair, having her hair cut. "When my grandson helped my husband decorate, we had a similar problem. Not so bad, mind, but it ended up the only thing that worked."

"Thank you," Max's mum said. "The chemist is close by; I'll nip and get a bottle, or a large one, or two, maybe." She spoke as she ran from the hair salon.

While Max waited for her mum to return, she had time to look in the large mirror and *really* see what she had done.

"Will you have to shave my head?" She twisted herself left and right to get a better idea. "Or, maybe, I can have one of those

Red Indian haircuts, a moccasin." *I quite fancy a look that matches the colour of my bike.*

"Mohican, not moccasin," Ant said, all helpful and big-brother clever. "You wear Moccasins on your feet."

The hairdresser seemed unsure about the conversation and the whole green hair idea. "I'm sure your school won't allow Mohican haircuts in class."

Max slumped back in her chair, "Grown-ups always spoil things," she muttered under her breath.

Max's mum burst through the salon door, "Here we are." She had rushed. "I got two large ones, just in case." She puffed.

"Okay, Max, over to the sink, please."

The hairdresser guided her to the hair-washing sink used before cutting. "Put this on to stop your clothes getting spoilt."

"Too late for that," Max's mum said with a resigned chuckle. "Everything's ruined. She has paint all over the house. Here, look at my hands." She held them out for everyone to see. "I need baby oil too." She shook her head in disbelief when she remembered the mess back at home. "What will your dad say young lady?"

Max lay back in the seat with her head over the sink. The hairdresser poured a large slurp of oil onto it and massaged it in.

"Shut your eyes," the hairdresser said.

Max scrunched her eyes tight to be certain. Slowly but surely, after repeated rubbing and slurping, the paint lost its grip on her hair. A green oily mixture gathered in the sink while more and more of Max's blonde hair colour returned.

"You've certainly hacked at this." The hairdresser prodded different clumps and tufts. "Most of this will have to come off."

"Does that mean I can have a Mohican?" Max sounded excited by the thought.

"What is she talking about? Mohican? Ant, did you put ideas in her head?" His mum stared at him.

"Don't blame me; she thought of it. She wanted a moccasin; I just told her it was a Mohican." Ant looked to the hairdresser for support.

"He's right, Mrs Turner. Anyway, I told

her the school wouldn't approve. Let's see what we can do."

The hairdresser led Max back to the large black swivel chair. After much clipping, snipping, combing, and pondering, the hairdresser had finished.

"Sorry, Mrs Turner; I've done my best."

Max looked in the mirror, as did her mum, and Ant.

"Well, at least it's an even length and one colour," her mum said.

"More like a baby hedgehog with short, soft blonde prickles." Ant smirked.

"Mum, tell him not to be nasty." Max lifted her hand to touch her head. All her life, she'd had long curly hair, and now it looked like nothing. She didn't say anything, but the quiver of her bottom lip gave away her true feelings. Her mum saw.

"It'll grow back in no time; you wait and see." Her mum smiled at her. "Now, tell you what, as we're here, I'll have a haircut, too. So, why don't you two pop to the café next to the chemist and get a cake and drink? I'll meet you there shortly." Their mum handed Ant a ten-pound note.

Between the hair salon and the café stood Ant's favourite shop—Boards and Bikes—it sold all things skateboarding and bikes. Whenever he went to the shopping centre, usually with Billy, they would stand outside the big window, staring in at all the different bits and wishing they had the money to buy them.

"Hey, Max, Mum will take a while; let's take a look inside?" Ant didn't wait for her to answer, and was first through the door. He headed for the skateboard display. Max followed but her interest lay in bikes.

She wandered up and down the aisles, looking at all the different models. Max liked the look of mountain bikes, but none resembled her newly painted one. Next to the bikes stood shelves of bits, spare parts, or new things that you could buy to make your bike better or different. She didn't understand most of them until she reached the display of stickers.

The shop had hundreds to choose from, in loads of colours and designs. Max picked through the clear plastic packets, and three caught her eye. One said, 'I Love My Bike', with a pink heart picture instead of the word love. The second said, 'Fast Bikes', with each letter in a different bold colour, including emerald green for the 'b' in bike. And the third said, 'No Fear'. *Hah, that would show Ant and Billy I can ride over their silly ramp.*

Max noticed herself in a bike mirror, the sort people use to see behind without turning around. As she stared at herself, her new look made her feel different, more determined, and more able to do boy's stuff. She did miss her old hair, but now, she felt less like a young child and more a nearly teenager. *I want those stickers,* kept running through her mind.

"Look, Ant, they only cost two pounds a packet." Max pushed them at him to see, but his focus stayed fixed on the skateboards. "Mum gave you a ten-pound note. Come on; she won't mind." Max punched his shoulder to get his attention while she held out the packets.

"You're joking, aren't you?" Ant turned to glance at them. "They look awesome, but you can't have them. Mum will go nuts if I let you have this money. After what you did with the paint, you'll lose your pocket money forever, I reckon." He put the skateboard wheel bearings he had been looking at back on the shelf. "Go on, return them; we'd better get to the café."

"Okaaay." Max stomped off. "It's not fair." Stopping at the end of the shelves where the rest of the stickers hung she slowly moved forward, while desperately trying to think of how she might get them even though she had no money. Before she realised it, she had slipped all three packets into her inside jacket pocket. Out of sight, no one could see them, she reasoned, and then told herself, *it'll be okay*. Max patted the outside of her jacket pocket; letting her thoughts go to cake and juice.

While she skipped to the door, she called out, "Come on, Ant."

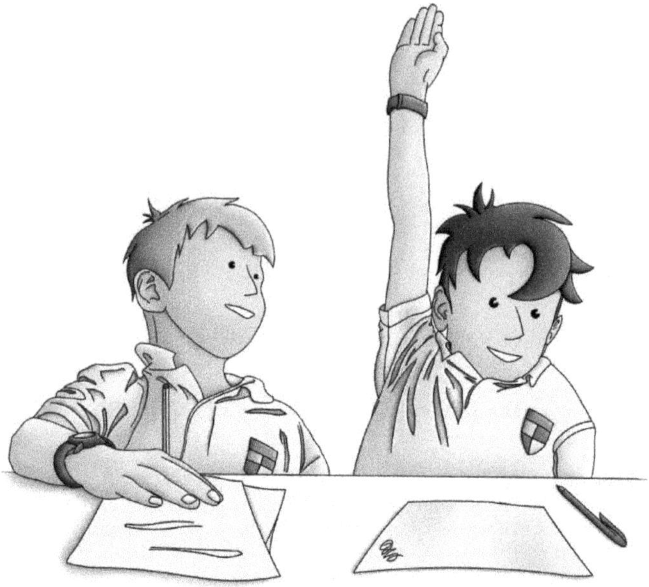

5

MAX SHARES A SECRET

Monday could not come quick enough for Max. Being at school had to be better than getting grounded with no one talking to her except about the green bike disaster.

Her mum dropped her at the school gate; Ant had ridden his bike. He stood at the bike shed with Billy and Tom—Katie's brother. Max could see them talking and pointing in her direction. As none of her classmates or anyone else at school had seen her new hair, she pulled her jacket collar up as high as it would go. She liked her hair but didn't want everybody seeing it at once and making silly remarks like hedgehog head or whatever Ant called her.

With each step across the playground, more and more children noticed until a small crowd of girls gathered around her.

"Why did you do that?" "Did it hurt?" "Can I touch it?" And other questions followed as she walked. She said nothing but smiled. Max saw Katie stood near the school door, she ran up to her.

"Crumbs, Max!" Katie slapped her hand to her mouth, confused by what she saw. "Tell me what happened, your hair looked normal on Saturday morning. I can't believe you've cut it all off."

The two girls pushed their way past the rest of the children and headed into the empty corridor.

"Remember, at your place last Saturday when I said *I'll show them*, and then jumped up and ran out" Max looked to Katie for a nod, "it happened after that. I went home and decided to paint my bike green. Well, not really. I would have liked yellow, but my dad only had green. ... The trouble is, it was gloss paint."

Katie looked puzzled.

Max continued. "Gloss isn't like school paint that washes off. Once you get gloss on your skin or clothes or hair or anywhere, it's almost impossible to get off." She took a gulp of air. "Somehow, I managed to paint my head right down my parting. It wouldn't wash off, so I tried to cut it out, and that's when my mum caught me in the bathroom."

"Do you mean your head went green?" Katie peered at Max's head to see if she could see any colour left on.

"Most of it, and my face. My jumper got soaked in paint, and I used it to wipe my face after a splash. Billy tried to help. He got this spirit stuff, it smelled all whiffy, but it cleaned my hands." Max held up her fingers. "Look, I still have green around my nails."

"You're unbelievable," Katie exclaimed. "Then what?"

"After that, Mum took me and Ant to the shopping centre to get my hair cut and head cleaned up."

"And? What else?" Katie wanted to hear the full story.

"I got grounded, and Dad went ballistic. He's fitted a big lock to his shed."

"What about your bike?"

"Gloss paint takes ages to dry. On Sunday, I wanted to put these on." Max pulled out the packets of stickers from her jacket pocket and passed them to Katie.

"I like this one best." Katie held up the *I Love My Bike* sticker. "I bet they cost you all your pocket money."

"They cost two pounds each."

"You had six pounds … wow!"

"Not really." Max looked around to see if anyone listened.

"What does *not really* mean?" Katie seemed confused.

Max moved close to Katie and whispered in her ear, "I didn't pay for them; they just sort of jumped into my pocket."

"Max! You know what you've done?" Katie took a step back.

"Shush; you've got to keep it a secret. Don't tell nobody. I'm in enough trouble as it is."

Burring, burring, burring … the school bell went.

"Come on; we've got to go in. Tell no one … promise." Max led Katie off to their classroom.

"Oi, Eddy." Katie got fed up with the noise he kept making. "I'm trying to watch telly," she shouted.

"You don't count, squirt, and I want to listen to this band." Eddy's music continued to blare out.

Tom sat at the table, trying to do his homework. "He'll go off out soon," he mouthed to Katie.

As if by magic, the music stopped. "See, I told you." Tom laughed.

"Well, good riddance." Katie huffed.

"Hey, what was that at school today with Max?" Tom asked.

"Didn't Billy or Ant tell you?" Katie turned to face him.

"Yeah, but you're Max's mate, and from what I hear, she got into real trouble. She splashed paint all around the house, and her bike's a right mess." Tom put his pencil down.

Katie stood and walked toward him. "Can you keep a secret?" She glanced about to make sure no one else was around.

"Of course." Tom sat up straight and pulled back his shoulders, "You can tell me anything."

Katie made her hand into a cup shape and placed it to his ear. "Max stole some stickers." She spoke in a whisper.

"What?"

"She stole some stickers for her bike …"

"Why? Where from?" Tom's eyebrows

shot into his hairline, and his eyes bulged. "Really?"

"Because she didn't have any money, and they cost six pounds, and she wanted her bike to look special." She stood back to look at Tom's face.

"But that's stealing! Everyone knows it's wrong to steal." Tom looked and sounded shocked.

"Shush. She made me promise not to tell anyone."

"Yeah, but she could get into bad trouble … with the police. You wait until I tell Ant." Tom looked determined.

"No, Tom, you can't."

"What else can we do? We can't just do nothing. Are you sure she stole them?"

"She told me herself." Katie now felt bad about telling him. "Please, don't tell Ant. Why don't you ask Billy what to do? He'll know."

Billy, Ant, and Tom had the same class and shared the same table at Grove Road primary school.

"Right, year five," Miss Tompkins, their form teacher, spoke to her students. "In this lesson, I want to talk about behaviour, and why good behaviour is important. I know most of you behave well most of the time, but just sometimes, one or two of you have let the class down." She looked around the group of faces staring back at her. "I won't pick on anyone, but this is a lesson about misbehaving, and how what you do affects others. ... Can anyone think of an example of misbehaving in class?" She waited for a show of hands.

"Swearing, Miss," Khalid called out without being asked.

"True, Khalid, but you've just broken an important class rule. Does anyone know what he did?" Miss Tompkins asked.

"Shouting out an answer without getting picked," Ant said.

Miss Tompkins stared at him, "Ant, I don't believe it. You've just done the same thing."

Everyone laughed.

"Sorry, Miss." Ant cast his eyes down.

Tom turned to Billy and whispered from

around the back of his hand, "Talking of bad behaviour; I need to tell you something about Max."

Billy screwed up his eyes and tilted his head. He opened his mouth to speak.

Before Billy could ask, Miss Tompkins spoke, "Tom, tell us another behaviour we must not do in class …"

"Sorry, Miss." Tom's face turned red.

"And tell the class, Tom, why you feel sorry."

"For whispering, Miss." Tom shuffled in his seat.

"Now, whispering isn't bad, but doing it in class when someone else is talking is rude behaviour. You disrespect the person speaking." Miss looked at her watch.

"Think about what we've said, and we'll continue the lesson after break."

In the playground, Billy turned to Tom, "What are you going on about?" Billy pulled Tom to one side, "Something about Max?" They moved to a corner of the playground.

Tom glanced round to see if Ant was close by. "Katie told me last night. We need to do something, or Max will get in even bigger trouble and maybe with the police!"

"Police, for painting your bike? No way." Billy grew even more confused.

"No, because Max stole some bike stickers; she showed them to Katie," Tom said. "She and Ant went to Boards and

Bikes, when she nicked three packets worth six pounds." Tom checked that Ant hadn't come near. "Ant knows nothing, so Katie thought, because you were there when she painted her bike, you could talk to Max."

"Why would she steal?" Billy rubbed his forehead, trying to think what to do. "Where is she?" He looked across the playground, she was easy to spot with her short hair. "Okay, I'll have a chat at lunchtime." Both boys headed back to their class.

"So, year five, we talked about bad behaviour ... remember." Miss Tompkins looked around the class, and everyone nodded.

"Yes, Miss," they all spoke together.

"Has anyone got a question?"

Tom nudged Billy. "Ask her about stealing," he mouthed.

"Ah, Tom," Miss Tompkins saw him. "Have you got something to say?"

"Not Tom, Miss, but I have," Billy answered for him. "I wondered about stealing, you know, if someone steals, what's the best thing to do?"

"Good question, Billy. I hope you've not stolen something."

The class laughed.

"Not me, Miss." Billy's face went red.

"Pleased to hear it." Miss Tompkins smiled. "Before I answer, we need to make sure that we know what stealing or theft is.

Any ideas?"

Everyone put up his or her hand.

"Khalid, glad to see your hand's up this time. So, what counts as stealing?" Miss Tompkins nodded to him.

"Nicking stuff, Miss."

"Can you say it any clearer, Khalid?"

"Taking things from other people."

"So, if I offered you a sweet, and you took it, is that stealing?"

"No, Miss. I meant taking things without asking. Like, if I went into a shop and stuffed sweets into my pocket and walked out without paying."

"That's better, Khalid. Stealing is taking things without permission or, if in a shop, without paying."

"But, Miss." Tom had his hand up. "It's sort of okay to take things from a shop because they've got loads."

"Absolutely not." Miss Tompkins sat upright in her chair. All the children knew that this meant she felt this too important a topic to move on. "Imagine what would happen if I took this class, all thirty of you, into a shop, and we each stole something. It would not take long before the shopkeeper would go out of business and have to close." She looked around to make sure they all listened to her. "The owner buys the items in the shop. He then sells them to customers. He uses the money from the sales to buy more things to sell." Miss Tompkins looked over the top her glasses to let her students know she was serious.

Billy sat with his hand raised.

"Billy, what's your question?" Miss Tomkins sounded abrupt.

"What if someone has already taken something from a shop, what should they do then?"

"Well, the person who stole needs to learn the lesson that it's wrong to steal. They need to return the goods to the shopkeeper and apologise for what they've done." Miss Tompkins watched his reaction, "Why do you ask, Billy?"

"Just wondering, Miss." Billy shot Tom a glance.

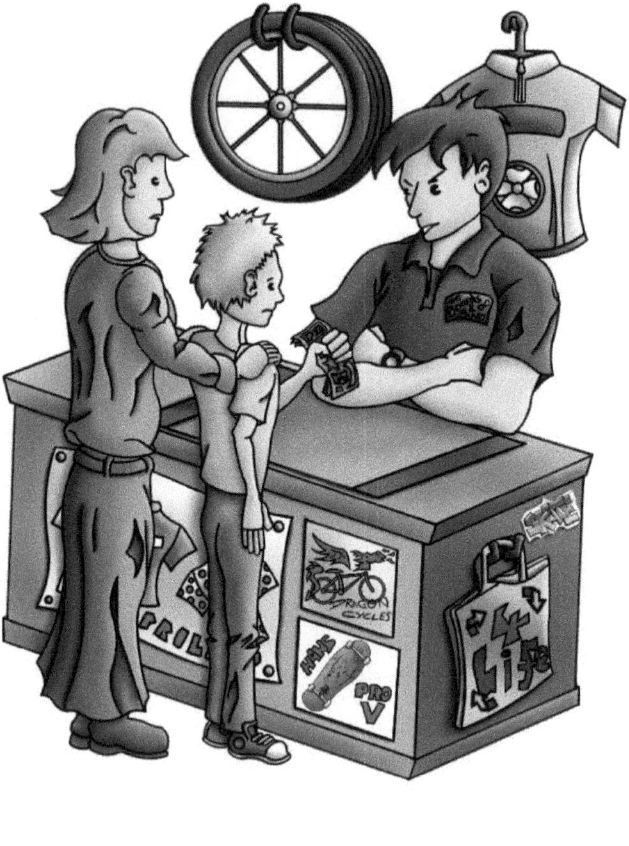
DRAGON CYCLES
HAWS
PRO V
4 Life

6

MAX OWNS UP TO STEALING

Billy finished his lunch as quickly as he could; he wanted to find Max as soon as possible. He glanced around the dining hall before dashing out to the playground. It didn't take him long to spot her.

"Max," Billy called out as he ran toward her. He reached her before she answered. "I need to talk to you, now." He huffed and puffed after his dash across the playground.

"Oh, hi, Billy." Max stopped talking to Katie and faced him, "What do you want?"

"Alone …" Billy looked at Katie.

Katie guessed Tom had talked to Billy, "See you in class, Max." She walked away.

Billy glanced around to make sure that no one could hear. "Someone told me you might be in real trouble." Billy looked at her, "And not for bike painting."

Max tried to look innocent, but ever since she had told Katie about stealing, she had grown worried. Unsure of what to do, she felt certain everyone knew her secret and were watching her.

Instead of owning up, Max tried to bluff, but her leg shook when she spoke, "I don't know what you mean."

Billy noticed. "You know … the bike stickers."

Now Max knew he knew she went red in the face and right down her neck. "Stickers?" Inside, her tummy did a tumble, and she felt scared. *If Billy knows, then who else does?* Panicked, she wanted to run away. Without thinking, she twisted herself sideways and stuck out one leg in readiness.

Billy saw and put a hand on her shoulder. "I want to help." He sounded kind.

"What can you do?" The feeling in her tummy lessened.

"I've talked to Miss Tompkins."

"She knows?" The panick feeling turned into a need to be sick.

"No, she doesn't know it's you," Billy said. "But we had a lesson on behaviour, and I asked a question about what should someone do if they have stolen something."

"What did she say?" Max frowned, not sure she wanted to know, but also curious to hear the answer.

"She said you need to put them back," Billy replied.

"Well, I sneaked them out of the shop, so I guess I can sneak them back again." It sounded easy. "Is that all?" Max smiled, hoping Billy would say yes.

"No, not quite."

Her smiley face changed back to scared.

"You need to apologise to the shop owner as well ... it's the way to learn that stealing is wrong, according to Miss."

"Yeah, but if I speak to him, he'll want to know my name, and he'll tell Mum and Dad." Max shook her head and folded her arms.

"So, that's why you have to tell your parents first," Billy said. "There's no other way."

Max's tummy did a double flip.

Back home from school, Max sat next to Ant at the tea table; neither spoke. Ant had talked earlier to Billy and knew what Max had to do. Their mum was stood nearby busy preparing a chilli-con-carne.

"So, how did school go?" Max's mum broke the silence. Like most parents she asked the same question every day, and like most children, Ant and Max answered in the same way with an "*okay.*"

"Everyone must have talked about your hair, Max." She looked at her daughter.

"They all wanted to stroke it like I was a dog." Max dropped her gaze to the table, wondering how she could tell her mum about stealing.

"And you, Ant?" Mum asked.

"Yeah, fine … when's Dad back? I'm starving."

"Soon. In the meantime, you two can talk to me." Their mum smiled as she spoke.

BILLY HELPS MAX

Ant pushed Max's arm. "Go on tell her," he whispered.

"No, get off me." Max turned away from him.

Ant persisted, "Better to do it now before Dad gets back."

"Do what?" Their mum had overheard.

"Nothing, Mum, Ant is just being annoying." Max pushed at his shoulder.

"She has something to tell you, Mum," Ant said.

Their mum noticed a tear fall from the corner of Max's eye, and her bottom lip wobble. "Max, dear, what is it? What happened? Did someone at school upset you? Come on love; you can tell your

Mum." Their mum walked over to her, bent down, and brought her face level with hers. "Do I need to go and speak to a teacher?"

"It's worse than that," Ant said, trying to be helpful again.

Max burst into tears, and her face turned bright red.

"Enough, Ant, no telling tales. Max can speak for herself." Her mum took a tissue from her pocket. "Here, blow your nose." Resting her arm on Max's shoulder, her mum waited for the burst of crying to stop. "So, what's so terrible?" Her mum wanted to stay calm, but all the time she had bad thoughts racing through her head.

"Stickers ... for my bike." Max squeezed the

words out; she found them difficult to say.

"What? You mean you want to buy some?" Her mum scowled. "Is that what this fuss is all about? You will get your pocket money again in a few weeks and not before. You're lucky it's no longer young lady, given what you've done."

"No, not buy. She stole some from the shopping centre," Ant declared.

"Stole? ... Stole? What do you mean "stole"?" Max's mum pulled out a chair. The shock felt too much. "When?"

With Ant's help, Max told her mum the whole story.

"And Billy said …" Ant added.

"Billy said. What does Billy know? Did he put her up to this?" Their mum looked at Max; she could not believe her little girl would have done such a thing.

"No, Mum, Billy's trying to help. Max needs to take them back to the shop, to own up to what she did, and apologise."

"Well, the sooner the better." Their mum sat thinking about what she had heard. "Right after school tomorrow."

On the bus, the journey from the school to the shopping centre took about ten minutes. Max sat on an inside seat nearest the window, and Ant sat beside her. Their mum sat right behind, watching her two children. Every now and then, she would shake her head in disbelief at what Max had done.

BILLY HELPS MAX

Max sat in a trance. She had been like it since teatime yesterday. Her mum knew it must all feel unreal, as if it had happened to someone else. Fear and guilt does that to people.

The bus stopped, and Ant stood. He tapped Max's shoulder, "Come on, sis. It won't take long. You'll see, it'll feel much better once you get it all over with." Ant took her hand and led her from the bus.

Max looked toward the entrance to the shopping centre, a shiver ran down her back. She wished she had never done it, but she had, and now she needed to put things right. When she reached the large glass doors, she saw Billy inside. Immediately, she felt better.

He understood things and wanted to help.

"Mum, there's Billy." She ran over to him, "Will you come with me, please Billy?"

He didn't speak; instead, he looked at Max's mum to see how she reacted to him.

Before he had time to make up his mind, Ant reached him. "Come on, mate." Ant said, "Max is off to see the shopkeeper at Boards and Bikes; remember what you told me?"

Max's mum seemed unsure whether it was a good idea for Billy to get involved. When they arrived at the Boards and Bikes shop, the three children hesitated outside and peered in. The shop had no customers, and only one man stood near the checkout.

"What will I say?" Max whispered.

"Say ..." Billy thought for a minute, "I need to bring these back, while you hand him the packets, and then tell him sorry for taking them without paying."

Max pushed on the shop door. Ant stood behind her, and Billy behind him. With glum faces they walked in a line; no one spoke. Their mum walked a few steps behind, ready to help if needed.

The shopkeeper looked up when he heard the door open and watched as the procession made its way toward him.

"Hi, kids. What can I do for you today?" The shopkeeper beamed, always pleased to see customers. "You don't look too happy. Any problem?" He directed his question toward Mum.

"Maxine, here—" She pointed at her daughter. "—has something to say."

"Well, Maxine, how can I help you?" The shopkeeper remained jolly.

"Please, Mister," Max started to speak, but her mouth felt dry, and the words stopped coming. She held out the packets of stickers.

The shopkeeper took them, "What are these?" He looked at each in turn, "Don't you like them?"

"No, it's not that …" Ant said.

"Shush, Ant, and let your sister speak," their mum said.

Max coughed and swallowed hard. "I …" She paused, and then said, "I took them without paying."

She spoke so softly that the shopkeeper didn't hear. "Sorry, Miss, can you say that again."

"I took them without paying." Max dropped her head forward and stared at the ground.

"You stole them!" The shopkeeper stood to his full height, pulling his shoulders back and pushing out his chest. He looked menacing and angry like he wanted to shout at her, as well as everyone else who had ever stolen from his shop.

He no longer appeared the happy, helpful person, but changed to a disappointed, hurt person. "What have I ever done to you to deserve this?"

Max felt guilty, and both Ant and Billy fidgeted in awkwardness, even though they hadn't done anything wrong.

"That's why we came here, to say sorry and return the stickers." Max's mum said to try and help out.

The shopkeeper glared at Max, then at her mum. "You are?"

"Mrs Turner." Max's mum held out her hand. "Maxine is my daughter."

Bewildered, the shopkeeper shook her hand. "What am I supposed to do? This should be a police matter. People who steal need stopping." The shopkeeper squatted down, bringing his eyes level with Max's. "I'm surprised at you. Why did you do it? If you were older, I would get the police involved, but you only seem …" He looked at Max's mum again.

"Eight," she said.

"Eight?" He said it once, then again, "Eight." He looked as if he couldn't believe it. Standing, he paced around his shop and rubbed his chin. "You're hardly out of nappies, and you're stealing. What's the world coming to?" He walked some more. "Well, at least you've owned up and returned the stickers." The shopkeeper looked sad. "That's more than most do."

"Max has something else to say." Her mum tapped Max's shoulder and mouthed "sorry."

"Sorry." Max sniffed so loudly that the shopkeeper didn't hear the word.

Her mum said, "Say it properly, Max."

"Sorry for taking the stickers without paying. I know it's wrong to steal." Tears streamed down her cheeks, and she shuffled from foot to foot.

"And?" her mum said.

"And, I promise I'll not to do it again." Max broke into uncontrollable crying. She ran to her mum and threw her arms around her.

"Well, I hope you've learned your lesson, young lady, and you too boys." The shopkeeper looked over at Ant and Billy, "I feel sure you won't get tempted to steal ... will you?"

They both shook their heads, "No, sir."

At school the next day, Mrs Johnston, the head teacher, took assembly. The whole school attended. Though she didn't mention Max by name, she talked about bad behaviours and stealing in particular.

Each time Mrs Johnston mentioned taking things without permission or without paying, Max felt a jolt in her stomach. It reminded her that she wouldn't get pocket money for a month, or be able to play with Katie, and she had extra things to do at home including feeding the rabbit, cleaning out its bedding, and sorting all the cans, bottles, and cardboard for recycling without any help from Ant.

Max's bike stood by her dad's shed where

she had left it to dry. She admired it, but without stickers or go-faster stripes, it looked unloved, forgotten, and abandoned. She remembered the day she had painted it, and then decided she didn't need to become like the boys. It was okay for her to be her.

"Hey, Max," Ant called from the other side of the garden. "Have you heard the rhyme about a bike? …

"Max has a bicycle
The colour of the grass.
Every time she tried to find it
She tripped and fell over it."

Max grunted at him and said, "Yeah, whatever."

"Okay, so not my funniest, but you try and make up a better one."

Max grinned at Ant's joke and realised she had been a bit hasty in thinking that repainting her bike would make her feel better. However, she would get over that much more quickly than how she felt about the stickers. She would never dare take anything again without asking or paying. Max breathed a sigh of relief—grateful for having listened to the boys' advice. They weren't so bad after all!

THE END

WHAT CHILDREN CAN LEARN FROM 'BILLY HELPS MAX'.

Stealing is taking another person's property without permission or payment, and without intending to return it. Most people have stolen something at one time or another, be it a pen from the office stationery cabinet, the soap from a hotel room, or not volunteered a bus fare. At the other end of the scale, people facing extreme hardship, steal food or other necessities for their family's survival because it offers the only option they have.

People see stealing in different ways. Stealing from a shop or company feels less impactful than stealing from an individual because we assume they have plenty. However, there are always consequences; if no one pays for the shop items, the shopkeeper will soon go out of business. There is also a type of stealing that may not be considered as stealing, such as acquiring someone else's idea like their music or their story. This proves especially true today with internet downloads, but it is still theft.

We may see a wallet left in a bus shelter and think that if we don't take it, someone else will, so we may as well take it. It's not until we stop and think about how the person who left the wallet will feel when they realise their loss, that we know that it's wrong and we should return it if at all possible or hand it in to the police.

But, for some people, stealing goes much further. It becomes a habit and can turn into a condition known as kleptomania — stealing things, even when they are not wanted or needed. People can also steal because they want to harm another person and watch them suffer; they get a sense of excitement or enjoyment from taking away something that's important to that person.

As in the story, Max knows that stealing is wrong but, at first, she justifies it to herself and even acts as if she just forgot to pay for the item. But stealing at whatever level is a crime, and if we get caught, there are serious consequences like fines or a prison sentence.

Parents can teach their children that

stealing is wrong by insisting they return whatever item they have taken and apologise to the owner. This makes the child understand that if they take something that doesn't belong to them, it impacts the other person and is wrong. Max was made aware that her only option was to return the item and apologise when her friend Billy pointed it out to her. She understood the ramifications of her actions.

Children especially are susceptible to getting persuaded by their peers to steal, perhaps by being dared to shoplift. This is part of learning how to deal with bullies who are able to manipulate vulnerable people. It is so hard in this case not to do as you're told, and so these types of people are best avoided. They have different values to you. And, always remember, if they steal from others, you can be sure they'll take every advantage to steal from you.

If you become the target of a theft, it can leave you with negative feelings of anger, loss, sadness, and frustration. The only thing to remember is that thieves do not care about how you feel, and so there is no point in thinking that they do. See if you can forgive and live your life knowing that bad people exist and that you are a better person than they are.

If we find ourselves stealing small items, it's worth thinking about why we needed to do that and explore the intention behind it. Is it because we feel life is unfair?

Because we feel sad, bored, or frustrated? Whatever the motive, there is never a good reason to steal anything from anyone.

I went to jail at 16 for stealing tyres off Cadillacs. When I got out, I said: Never again — **Barry White**

No one likes to work for free. To copy an artist's work and download it free is stealing. It's hard work writing and recording music, and it's morally wrong to steal it — **Gary Wright**

There was one 'crime" during the whole time I was at school when a fountain pen went missing. I was taught not to shoplift, not to steal, not to behave badly. We weren't even allowed to drop litter — **Joanna Lumley**

GET YOUR FREE ACTIVITY BOOK

To accompany all the Billy Books there is a free activity book for each title. Each book includes word search, crossword, secret message, maze and cryptogram puzzles plus pictures to colour.

To get your **free** Activity Book go to **www.thebillybooks.co.uk** and click the button **Get Your Free Activity Book**. Then click the cover of the book matching this book

BOOK REVIEW

If you found this book helpful, leaving a review on Goodreads.com or other book related websites would be much appreciated by me and others who have yet to find it.

READ ON FOR A TASTER
OF

BILLY SAVES THE DAY

BILLY GROWING UP SERIES:

SELF-BELIEF

James Minter

Helen Rushworth - Illustrator

www.billygrowingup.com

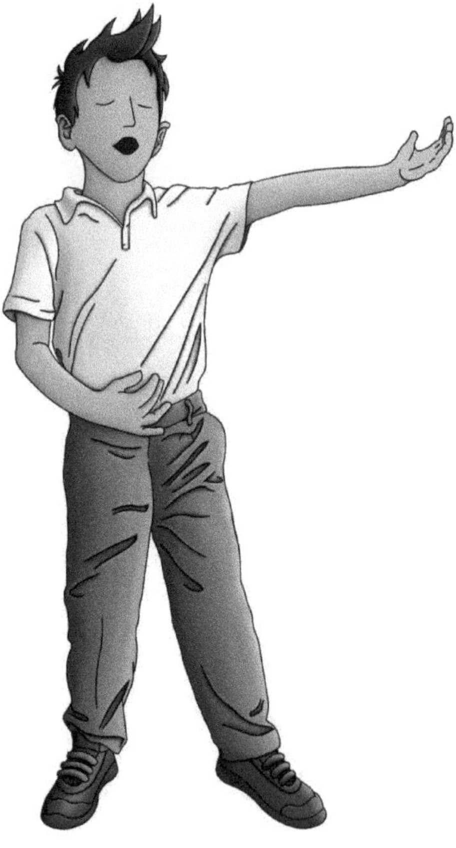

1

END-OF-YEAR PRODUCTION

Miss Tompkins, Billy's year five form teacher, passed around a pile of books — play scripts. "Please, take a copy … quickly and quietly. "She watched until each child had one. "Now, turn to page two and read the section headed *Director's Overview.*" Miss Tompkins stared at the class over the top of her glasses; she appeared severe and rather scary. As each child noticed, they fell silent and read. Nobody liked being called out for talking or not doing their work.

"Miss … " Khalid said.

"Khalid, how many more times; no shouting out. Put your hand up first." She scowled.

"Sorry, Miss." He pretended to zip his lips before raising his hand.

"Yes, Khalid, what's your question?"

"Why are we reading this?" Khalid waved around his copy of the script.

"Good question. Can anyone help him?" Miss gazed at her class. Three hands went up, including Tom's. "So, Tom, what do you think?"

"For our year-end production." Tom sat back in his chair, folded his arms across his chest, and beamed a smile.

BILLY SAVES THE DAY

Tom shared a table with his two best mates Billy and Ant.

"We all knew that." Ant spoke around the back of his hand so that Miss would not hear.

Miss Tompkins spoke, "We have eight weeks until you finish in year five and move into the last year at this school, and by tradition, we will entertain the whole school with a play. This year, we shall perform The Keymaster by Nick Perrin. From reading the overview, you should know that it's about time travel, going back in history, to 1066 and other important dates." Miss Tompkins saw a hand go up. "Yes, Billy."

"But, Miss, it's a musical with singing

and stuff. That'll be hard." Billy looked to Ant and Tom for support. They both nodded.

"Well, Billy, you are near the end of your time in year five, as are you all, and from my experience, I think you'll do a great job, possibly the best by a year five class." Miss Tompkins stood and walked around to the front of her desk. "We need to cast; that means choose who will play which part. We also need scenery painting, costumes sewing, and props making. This production will involve the whole class, and for the main characters, rehearsals will happen late afternoon, once school has finished."

A buzz of excitement came from the

children, and Khalid burst into song, "Doe, ray, me fa, so, la, ti, doeeeeee." He held the last note for as long as he could.

"Okay, Khalid." Miss Tompkins clapped her hands, "You will have plenty of time for that. For the rest of this lesson and homework, I would like you to read the whole script and decide who you would like to be. If several people want the same part, like the Keymaster or one of the other four leading roles, we will need to hold auditions, or I will have to choose."

Billy, Ant, and Tom rode their bikes home after school, chatting all the time about the end-of-year play.

"Yeah, but I'm the creative one," Ant

boasted. "Miss always says so. Remember how I won the prize for the advert project at the end of the last term." Ant pushed out his chest. "It should be me who plays the Keymaster." He looked to Billy and Tom, expecting to see them agree.

"But the Keymaster is meant to be a teacher who turns into a time traveller," Tom said. He sat upright on his bike to show how grown up he was. Speaking in his best gruff dad's voice, "So, I should play that part. I'm the tallest and look more like a grown-up."

"Maybe," Billy said. "But Khalid has a good singing voice. You heard him in class doing his doe, ray, mi thing."

"True, but when Khalid speaks, he looks

down a lot, and Miss won't like that," Ant said. "When you're on stage, you have to look out at the audience and speak slowly and clearly." Ant spoke slowly and clearly to emphasise what he meant.

The three boys stopped at the road crossing; the red man showed. Ant pressed the button.

"You need to get off and push your bike," Ant called—he could see two mums with pushchairs waiting to cross from the other side.

The red man changed to green, and the familiar beep, beep, beep sound signalled it was safe to go. "Come on, you two." Ant set off toward the far side. Only after he had crossed did he notice that Billy and

Tom hadn't followed him.

"Oi, you two, get a move on," Ant called back to them.

For Billy and Tom, it proved too late; the green man had changed back to red, and the traffic started moving. Ant watched and tried to speak to them, but the car noise made it impossible.

🐕 🐕

"So, what do you think?" Billy asked Tom. "Should the Keymaster be Ant or Khalid?"

"I've not heard Ant sing. I don't know if he can." Tom still thought he should get cast as Keymaster. "Ant is good at telling jokes," Tom said. He didn't want to say anything bad about Ant since they were mates, but neither did he want to help him get the part.

The beep, beep, beep sound of the crossing made Billy and Tom look up. They saw Ant across the road, waving his arms like a windmill in a storm.

"Yeah, we're coming," Billy called to him. He turned to Tom and said, "Say nothing to Ant. I want to read the play again to decide what I'll do, but I know I'm all right with a hammer, nails, and a paint brush; maybe I'll just build scenery."

"What? Build scenery? You should go on stage, get a speaking part—"

Billy interrupted Tom, "Singing, don't you mean?"

"Okay, a singing part, but whatever, you should act. Miss will expect you to." Tom patted Billy on the back. "You wait."

"Yeah, but I'll be no good." Billy slumped his shoulders and looked at the ground as he spoke; he didn't want Ant or Tom to see his face. Billy felt awkward, swallowed up by embarrassment.

Because he'd looked down, Billy missed the surprised expression on Tom's face.

"You're nuts, Billy Field. You're one of the best in class."

Billy didn't share Tom's confidence in himself. *Yeah, but what do you know?* He thought.

As usual, Billy and Ant cycled the rest of the way home together. They arrived outside Ant's house. Although Billy lived two streets away from Ant, after school, Billy went to his grandad's to wait for his mum to get home from work. His grandad lived just two houses away from Ant.

"See ya, mate." Ant waved goodbye to Billy and then disappeared into his garden. Ant had spotted his mum and younger sister, Max, at the rabbit hutch. Max, still grounded, had to do extra jobs after her bike-painting episode a couple of weeks earlier, when she'd managed to cover herself, and all around the house, in green gloss paint.

"Hi, Mum. Hi, sis." Ant parked his bike against the house wall. He dropped his school bag, his high-vis jacket, and cycle helmet, and then sprinted over to see

Cinders, their pet rabbit.

"Careful with her. Hold her under the back legs; otherwise, she'll kick," Ant's mum said.

"Hello, Cinders," Ant stroked the rabbit's long grey-flecked ears. He watched as she twitched her nose. "What can you smell?" He put his fingers near her face; she sniffed them before trying to nibble on one.

"Oi, no, they're not carrots, they're my fingers." Ant snatched his hand away; her teeth looked sharp, and he didn't want her to bite him.

Max opened the door to the rabbit run. "Here, Ant, put her back. She has clean water, fresh straw for her bed, and a bunch of lettuce leaves."

"How was school?" His mum asked Ant the usual question.

"Fine, I suppose." Ant gave his usual answer.

"Just fine?" His mum had hoped for more.

"We're doing an end-of-year play … something about time travel. I've got to read the script to decide who to be."

"I'm sure you can play whoever you want, my little actor." His mum leaned over to give him a hug, and then kissed the top of his head.

"But, we have to sing … it's a musical." Ant looked up at her before wriggling free.

"Sing! I've never heard you sing except for Baa, Baa Black Sheep or Twinkle,

Twinkle Little Star, and that was years ago. Knowing you, I'm sure you'll manage to do it; my Ant can do anything." His mum hugged him a second time.

I HOPE YOU ENJOYED THIS FREE CHAPTER. TO FIND OUT WHAT HAPPENS NEXT PLEASE READ 'BILLY SAVES THE DAY.'

FOR PARENTS, TEACHERS, AND GUARDIANS: ABOUT THE 'BILLY GROWING UP" SERIES

Billy and his friends are children entering young adulthood, trying to make sense of the world around them. Like all children, they are confronted by a complex, diverse, fast-changing, exciting world full of opportunities, contradictions, and dangers through which they must navigate on their way to becoming responsible adults.

What underlies their journey are the values they gain through their experiences. In early childhood, children acquire their values by watching the behaviour of their parents. From around eight years old onwards, children are driven by exploration, and seeking independence; they are more outward looking. It is at this age they begin to think for themselves, and are capable of putting their own meaning to feelings, and the events and experiences they live through. They are developing their own identity.

The Billy Books series supports an initiative championing Values-based Education, (VbE) founded by Dr Neil Hawkes*. The VbE objective is to influence a child's capacity to succeed in life by encouraging them to adopt positive values that will serve them during their early lives, and sustain them throughout their adulthood. Building on the VbE objective, each Billy book uses the power of traditional storytelling to contrast negative behaviours with positive outcomes to illustrate, guide, and shape a child's understanding of the importance of values.

This series of books help parents, guardians and teachers to deal with the issues that challenge children who are coming of age. Dealt with in a gentle way through storytelling, children begin to understand the challenges they face, and the importance of introducing positive values into their everyday lives. Setting the issues in a meaningful context helps a child to see things from a different perspective. These books act as icebreakers, allowing easier communication between parents, or other significant adults, and children when it comes to discussing difficult subjects. They are suitable for KS2, PSHE classes.

There are eight books are in the series. Suggestions for other topics to be dealt with in this way are always welcome. To this end, contact the author by email: james@jamesminter.com.

*Values-Based Education, (VbE) is a programme that is being adopted in schools to inspire adults and pupils to embrace and live positive human values. In English schools, there is now a Government requirement to teach British values. More information can be found at: www.valuesbasededucation.com/

BILLY GETS BULLIED

Bullies appear confident and strong. That is why they are scary and intimidating. Billy loses his birthday present, a twenty-pound note, to the school bully. With the help of a grown-up, he manages to get it back and the bully gets what he deserves.

BILLY AND ANT FALL OUT

False pride can make you feel so important that you would rather do something wrong than admit you have made a mistake. In this story, Billy says something nasty to Ant and they row. Ant goes away and makes a new friend, leaving Billy feeling angry and abandoned. His pride will not let him apologise to his best friend until things get out of hand.

BILLY IS NASTY TO ANT

Jealousy only really hurts the person who feels it. It is useful to help children accept other people's successes without them feeling vulnerable. When Ant wins a school prize, Billy can't stop himself saying horrible things. Rather than being pleased for Ant, he is envious and wishes he had won instead.

BILLY AND ANT LIE

Lying is very common. It's wrong, but it's common. Lies are told for a number of different reasons, but one of the most frequent is to avoid trouble. While cycling to school, Billy and Ant mess around and lie about getting a flat tyre to cover up their lateness. The arrival of the police at school regarding a serious crime committed earlier that day means their lie puts them in a very difficult position.

BILLY HELPS MAX

Stealing is taking something without permission or payment. Children may steal for a dare, or because they want something and have no money, or as a way of getting attention. Stealing shows a lack of self-control. Max sees some go-faster stripes for her bike. She has to have them, but her birthday is ages away. She eventually gives in to temptation.

BILLY SAVES THE DAY

Children need belief in themselves and their abilities, but having an inflated ego can be detrimental. Lack of self-belief holds them back, but overpraising leads to unrealistic expectations. Billy fails to audition for the lead role in the school play, as he is convinced he is not good enough.

BILLY WANTS IT ALL

The value of money is one of the most important subjects for children to learn and carry with them into adulthood, yet it is one of the least-taught subjects. Billy and Ant want skateboards, but soon realise a reasonable one will cost a significant amount of money. How will they get the amount they need?

BILLY KNOWS A SECRET

You keep secrets for a reason. It is usually to protect yourself or someone else. This story explores the issues of secret-keeping by Billy and Ant, and the consequences that arise. For children, the importance of finding a responsible adult with whom they can confide and share their concerns is a significant life lesson.

MULTIPLE FORMATS

Each of the Billy books is available as a **paperback**, as a **hardback** including coloured pictures, as **eBooks** and in **audio**-book format.

COLOURING BOOK

The Billy Colouring book is perfect for any budding artist to express themselves with fun and inspiring designs. Based on the Billy Series, it is filled with fan-favourite characters and has something for every Billy, Ant, Max and Jacko fan.

THE BILLY BOOKS COLLECTIONS VOLUMES 1 AND 2

For those readers who cannot wait for the next book in the series, books 1, 2, 3, and 4 are combined into a single work — The Billy Collection, Volume 1, whilst books 5, 6, 7, and 8 make up Volume 2.

The collections are still eligible for the free activity books. Find them all at www.thebillybooks.co.uk .

ABOUT THE AUTHOR

I am a dad of two grown children and a stepfather to three more. I started writing five years ago with books designed to appeal to the inner child in adults - very English humour. My daughter Louise, reminded me of the bedtime stories I told her and suggested I write them down for others to enjoy. I haven't yet, but instead, I wrote this eight-book series for 7 to 9-year-old boys and girls. They are traditional stories dealing with negative behaviours with positive outcomes.

Although the main characters, Billy and his friends, are made up, Billy's dog, Jacko, is based on our much-loved family pet, which, with our second dog Malibu, caused havoc and mayhem to the delight of my children and consternation of me.

Prior to writing, I was a college lecturer and later worked in the computer industry, at a time before smartphones and tablets, when computers were powered by steam and stood as high as a bus.

WEBSITES

www.billygrowingup.com

www.thebillybooks.co.uk

www.jamesminter.com

E-MAIL

james@jamesminter.com

TWITTER

@james_minter

@thebillybooks

FACEBOOK

facebook.com/thebillybooks/

facebook.com/author.james.minter

ACKNOWLEDGEMENTS

Like all projects of this type, there are always a number of indispensable people who help bring it to completion. They include Christina Lepre, for her editing and incisive comments, suggestions and corrections. Harmony Kent for her proofreading, and Helen Rushworth of Ibex Illustrations, for her images that so capture the mood of the story. Gwen Gades for her cover design. And Maggie, my wife, for putting up with my endless pestering to read, comment and discuss my story, and, through her work as a personal development coach, her editorial input into the learnings designed to help children become responsible adults.

IBEX ILLUSTRATIONS